Baby Lamb

By Beth Spanjian
Illustrated by John Butler

A GOLDEN BOOK • NEW YORK
Western Publishing Company, Inc., Racine, Wisconsin 53404

Text © 1988 Angel Entertainment, Inc. Illustrations © 1988 John Butler. All rights reserved. First published by Longmeadow Press. Printed in the U.S.A. No part of this book may be reproduced or copied in any form without written permission from the publisher. GOLDEN, GOLDEN & DESIGN, GOLDENCRAFT, A GOLDEN BOOK, A GOLDEN LOOK-LOOK BOOK, and A GOLDEN LOOK-LOOK BOOK & DESIGN are trademarks of Western Publishing Company, Inc. Library of Congress Catalog Card Number: 90-81293 ISBN: 0-307-12604-8/ ISBN: 0-307-62602-4 (lib. bdg.)
MCMXCI

It is a crisp spring morning. A rooster's crow breaks the silence. The dew on a neatly spun spiderweb sparkles in the sunlight. Nestled in clean straw, Baby Lamb and her twin brother begin their day.

The two little lambs are hungry. They nudge their mother with their small black faces and find her warm milk. Baby Lamb's stubby tail wags back and forth as she fills her empty stomach.

Baby Lamb's mother and the other ewes stare through the fence toward the house, looking for any sign of the farmer. Soon, he comes with his arms full of fresh alfalfa hay.

While their mothers pull the hay from the feeder, the little lambs romp and play in the pen. Baby Lamb playfully kicks up her heels. It is such a beautiful spring day!

Today is shearing day. The ewes' woolly coats have grown long and thick. The farmer rests Baby Lamb's mother against his knees and carefully shears her fleece all in one piece.

Soon Mother is back with Baby Lamb and her brother. She seems very skinny without her thick wool coat!

Suddenly, the gate to the sheep pen flies open, and in runs the farmer's sheepdog. The sheep flock together, baaing and bleating. The dog herds the sheep out through the gate and toward the pasture.

Baby Lamb runs ahead and loses sight of her mother. "Baaaa, Baaaa," she cries. Her mother calls back, and soon the family of three is together again.

It is Baby Lamb's first time in the pasture. She nibbles at the tender grass, and surprises a butterfly.

Baby Lamb and her playmates watch as the farmer walks along the fence, checking it for holes. The lambs cautiously follow the man and his dog from post to post.

Evening has come and Baby Lamb's mother lies quietly in the grass, chewing her cud. The two little lambs nestle beside her until morning, when they will wake with the sun!

Facts About Baby Lamb (A Suffolk Sheep)

Where Do Lambs Live?

Sheep are raised in every state of the Union, yet seventeen western states produce about eighty percent of the sheep in the United States. California and Texas are the leading sheep producers. Sheep are usually raised in flocks of one thousand or more on the open range, or in small farm flocks of up to five hundred. Domestic sheep have lost the ability to protect themselves, so many ranchers rely on sheepherders or watchdogs to protect them from coyotes or stray dogs.

What Do Lambs Eat?

Though young lambs feed on their mother's milk, grown sheep eat grass—and lots of it! When a pasture is covered with snow, or not growing, farmers and ranchers must feed sheep hay. They may also feed them grain to fatten them for market. Sheep are known as "ruminants," because their stomachs have four chambers. They "chew their cud," which means that once they swallow their food, they bring it back up into their mouths later for a second, more thorough chewing, before they digest it.

How Do Lambs Communicate?

Sheep communicate with each other with "baas," "maas" and other bleating sounds. They can recognize each other's voices, which helps keep the lambs from getting lost. Mothers can detect their young by smell.

How Big Are Lambs, and How Long Do They Live?

Sheep come in all sizes and shapes. Dozens of breeds exist in America. Most sheep are white, but some have black, gray or brown wool. Some breeds of sheep, such as Suffolk, Hampshire and Dorset, are best known for their tasty meat. Other sheep, like Lincolns, Merinos and Rambouillets, are best known for their wool. Sheep can live up to eight years, and some even longer.

What Is A Lamb's Family Like?

Mother sheep (called ewes) have one or two lambs each winter, though triplets aren't rare. People who raise sheep usually keep father sheep (called rams) away from the ewes, except during the fall for breeding. This way, ranchers can control when the lambs are born. Ewes give birth to their young five months after breeding, often in February. The newly born lambs are usually on their feet and nursing within minutes. The lambs are born with long, spindly tails that are later shortened so they don't grow thick and heavy with dirt.

What Are Lambs Raised For?

Sheep are raised for their meat, wool, milk, leather and lanolin, an oil used to make soaps and lotions. Lambs raised for meat grow fast and put on muscle quickly, but usually produce low-quality wool. Sheep raised for wool may produce a fleece that weighs four times more than the fleece of another breed of sheep. For instance, a Suffolk sheep, raised for its meat may grow a five-pound fleece, while a Merino sheep, raised for its wool, may grow a twenty-pound fleece! Some sheep are raised for their milk, which is then made into cheese.